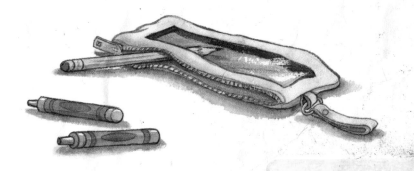

Biscuit
Goes to School

story by ALYSSA SATIN CAPUCILLI
pictures by PAT SCHORIES

HarperCollinsPublishers

HarperCollins®, 🐾®, and I Can Read Book® are trademarks of HarperCollins Publishers Inc.

Biscuit Goes to School Text copyright © 2002 by Alyssa Satin Capucilli Illustrations copyright © 2002 by Pat Schories All rights reserved. No part of this book may be used or reproduced in any manner whatsoever without written permission except in the case of brief quotations embodied in critical articles and reviews. Printed in the United States of America. For information address HarperCollins Children's Books, a division of HarperCollins Publishers, 1350 Avenue of the Americas, New York, NY 10019. www.harpercollinschildrens.com

Library of Congress Cataloging-in-Publication Data

Capucilli, Alyssa.
    Biscuit goes to school / story by Alyssa Satin Capucilli ; pictures by Pat Schories.
        p.   cm.—(A my first I can read book)
    Summary: A dog follows the bus to school, where he meets the teacher and takes part in the activities of the class.
    ISBN-10: 0-06-028682-2 (trade bdg.) — ISBN-13: 978-0-06-028682-8 (trade bdg.)
    ISBN-10: 0-06-028683-0 (lib. bdg.) — ISBN-13: 978-0-06-028683-5 (lib. bdg.)
    ISBN-10: 0-06-443616-0 (pbk.) — ISBN-13: 978-0-06-443616-8 (pbk.)
    [1. Dogs—Fiction. 2. Schools—Fiction.] I. Schories, Pat, ill. II. Title. III. Series.
PZ7.C179Bisf 2002   00-049881
[E]—dc21   CIP
                                                                                                       AC

❖

For the wonderful students, teachers, librarians, and parents who have welcomed Biscuit into their schools!

Here comes the school bus!
Woof, woof!

Stay here, Biscuit.

Dogs don't go to school.

Woof!

Where is Biscuit going?

Is Biscuit going to the pond?

Woof!

Is Biscuit going to the park?

Woof!

Biscuit is going to school!
Woof, woof!

Biscuit wants to play ball.

Woof, woof!

Biscuit wants
to hear a story.
Woof, woof!
Shhh!

Biscuit wants a snack.

Woof, woof!

Oh, Biscuit!

What are you doing here?

Dogs don't go to school!

Oh, no!

Here comes the teacher!

Woof!

Biscuit wants

to meet the teacher.

Woof!

Biscuit wants
to meet the class.
Woof, woof!

Biscuit likes school!

Woof, woof!

And everyone at school
likes Biscuit!
Woof!